Pokemon Go: Diary Of A Pokemon Trainer

Copyright © 2016 @ Red Smith

(An Unofficial Pokémon Book)

Second Edition

How to Become a Legendary Pokémon Trainer in your Space!

Quickly Access the Ideal Strategies & techniques to Catch Rare Pokémon's

Here's how you Take Over Gyms and Mark your Territory...

Don't Waste your time, invest it wisely and learn the Best Strategies, Ultra Unique Techniques and Best Kept Secrets for Leveling up in Pokémon Go.

Sign Up here to be the first in line: www.smarturl.it/PokemonGuide

Become the Ultimate Trainer in your Area!

Find out about optimal strategies to catch rare Pokémon~!

Increase chance to catch Rare Pokemon

Mark your Territory and Never let Trainers dominate you

CP **1650**

Golem

Read the most Updated Guide on Amazon Now

Are you Ready to become the Master?

Subscribe your Email to be notified first!

www.smarturl.it/PokemonGuide

MONDAY

The cry of a Pidgey woke me up way too early. But, if it hadn't been for that wild pokemon sitting outside of my window, Mom would have been running in, waking me up.

"Get out of bed! It's already after 8!"

Too late, Mom. A Pidgey – that I have yet to catch – beat you to it.

So, I crawled out of my bed. I knew I had a lot to do today, but I did not want to deal with my social life.

My
dream...

I knew training to become a pokemon master wouldn't be easy. And I knew it would take a lot of hard work, which hey, I am willing to do. But, I didn't think life would be so hard. Whenever I try to train alone, or even try catching a pokemon, that burly idiot Scott won't leave me alone. Indian burns, wet willies, general abuse. I thought I would try to one up him with some reverse psychology, because clearly he's not too smart, but whenever I try to trick him, he just hits me. Maybe I should just practice running. If I get fast enough, I can run from Scott, or even a Gyarados. Or maybe I should find a Magikarp and raise it to be a Gyarados... then he wouldn't mess with me at all! His real colors would show... he'd be a real chicken.

And as if Scott wasn't bad enough... I have a HUGE crush on Misty – but I have no idea how to tell her! She's so pretty, smart, and a WAY better pokemon trainer than me. She's already got a Pikachu. I just have a Rattata and a Caterpie! Total weaklings, just like me. Misty is a total inspiration for me to become a real pokemon master. Misty would like me if I had a full pokedex, right?

"Your breakfast is getting cold! I won't cook you anything else! And make your bed!"

My Rattata and Caterpie!

Sshhh...I have a HUGE crush on Misty

Blah, blah, blah. Always nagging! Between Mom's nagging and Dad's constant "advice" about pokemon training, it's exhausting. I know deep down that Mom loves me, but calm down, crazy lady. And as for Dad... I get it. You catch Moltres, travel across the world to catch pokemon, and earn all those badges, and you think you're hot stuff. Like, I know I have to fill his shoes. And the hardest part... he's so patient. He's not pushy, and he doesn't make me feel stupid. How can I be angry at him?

That's what we're working on today. Catching. I always get too excited, and scare off whatever pokemon I'm trying to catch. Dad says I have to be more quiet... to embrace the moment. He says that, later this week, we're going to work on battles. Like he has a pokemon young enough to make it an even battle with my Rattata. It'd be like a horror movie! Maybe if I work hard enough, I could have a battle with Scott. I think all he has is a Bulbasaur. Maybe I can find a Charmander and whip him around. Put him in his place. It'd be fixing three problems at once! I'd put Scott in his place, Misty would HAVE to notice me... and then I'd win my first battle. I guess I just have to eat breakfast first. I'll check back later!

MONDAY NIGHT

I'm exhausted, but the hard work with Dad paid off this afternoon. I caught a Bulbasaur! What an awesome end to a very long day. Before we walked off into the woods, Dad took hours showing me how to be sneaky when it comes to catching a pokemon. Who would have thought that you couldn't just run up to one, expecting it to battle? Plus, you have to THINK like a pokemon. Depending on the type, the pokemon might be more playful. Or it might be scared. You have to know your stuff, and think with your gut.

After the very long lesson, I decided I felt ready enough to take Rattata out to the field close to our house. Dad led me there, explaining what types of pokemon are known to run around in the field. Uh, duh, Dad. I knew that already. I've been waiting to catch a Bulbasaur since I was in diapers.

But, I was also nervous. With Rattata and Caterpie, I got very lucky. I caught them by accident! I took some pokeballs from Dad's office, and walked to the edge of the field. I knew if I got caught, I'd be in big trouble. Dad had always told me to NEVER go to the field alone, so I knew it was dangerous... but I really wanted a pokemon. I had to show up that bully, Scott. Right as I was walking up to the field, my Rattata just walked out of the field. He looked so cute... I just tossed a ball and he hopped in. It was fate, it had to be. As I walked home, grinning from ear to ear, I noticed Caterpie hanging on a tree branch. I thought I couldn't be that lucky, getting a second pokemon in one day. But I was.

When we got to the edge of the field this time, Dad asked if I was ready. Of course I was!

We walked through the tall grass... and I really didn't see too much at first. But then, I heard Dad whisper, "To your left."

There he was. A Bulbasaur. MY Bulbasaur. I remembered my training from this afternoon. At first, I just kind of watched him. Eventually, he noticed me. Bulbasaur started to move towards me. I was so happy! I started reaching for a ball, and Dad whispered, "Not yet. You have to earn his trust." How was I supposed to do that?!

We got closer. I looked into Bulbasaur's eyes. He's one of my favorite pokemon, out of ALL of them. Suddenly, I felt a connection to the little green guy. And I think he felt it, too. We just kind of looked at each other, for what felt like forever. Eventually, I felt Dad's hand on my shoulder. That meant it was time.

I reached for a pokeball, said a quick prayer, and threw it. AND I CAUGHT IT!

For the first time ever, I feel like I can really do this. I really can become a great pokemon master, just like Dad. I can fill my pokedex, travel the world, get Misty to like me (I hope…), and work up the courage to challenge Scott to a pokemon battle that I will then win. I can pull it off! But first... I need some sleep.

Yeah...I caught a Bulbasaur!

Tuesday Night

Mom and Dad always taught me that hate is a strong word, and I shouldn't use it.

But guess what? I really, really, really, really, really cannot stand Scott. He is kind of the worst human being ever. I would rather be stuck in a small room with an untamed Charizard.

I was so proud of catching a Bulbasaur. Duh! It's a big accomplishment for me. So, earlier this morning, I ran off to tell my friends about how I caught one of the coolest pokemon ever. But of course, Scott found me first.

"What kind of a dweeb would be excited about catching a weak little Bulbasaur? You can't beat anything with that! You might as well fight me with a Rattata!"

Great. You just can't win with this guy.

After a few punches, he let me leave. And of course, Misty was hanging out with my usual group of friends when I walked up.

"What happened to you? Are you okay?!" Misty was the first one from the group to run to me. My heart did this weird flip-flop thing. Emotions are weird.

"I ran into Scott. He didn't like the fact that I caught a Bulbasaur. He called me weak."

"You caught a Bulbasaur? That's AWESOME!" Misty shouted. "He's a loser if he can't see what an accomplishment that is. He's just mad because he can't get anywhere with his one Pidgey. You should be so proud of yourself. I know I'm proud of you."

My heart was BEATING in my chest now. She thinks I'm cool! She's proud of me! I'm finally making strides to get to know Misty, rather than just watching her from far away. I know that sounds really creepy, but I promise it's not. I just like her.

"Have you had your first battle yet?"

Oh, those words. Of course I haven't... I'm nowhere near ready to have my first battle. I only have three pokemon! I panic. I want to look cool... but I don't want to lie.

"Not yet," I replied. "Dad is working with me to make sure my first battle ends with a win."

"You are SO lucky," Misty said. "Your dad is a legend! With him teaching you, I know you could be an even better pokemon trainer than him."

I feel like I'm going to throw up, in the best possible way

you could imagine. She thinks I can be better than DAD?! Is she just being nice... or does she like me? I'll never understand girls, but Misty is the only girl who can make me want to throw up. In a happy way...

So, I'm covered in bruises, but I've never been happier. My Bulbasaur is hanging out in his new home. Misty thinks I'm the COOLEST, which duh, of course I am. And tomorrow, Dad and I are working on my first battle. He says he has a young Nidoran that we can train with Bulbasaur. He also says that I can't favor just one pokemon – I have to train them equally. So, maybe Rattata and Caterpie will see some action tomorrow, too!

I'm nervous... but I've also never been this excited! Tomorrow will be amazing. With Dad by my side, and with my young pokemon with me... I'm destined to win. I'm destined to be as good as my dad.

WEDNESDAY

Okay. I'm not destined to win. I am destined to be awful.

Think of everything that can go wrong during a battle... and it happened to me today.

I can tell that Bulbasaur and I have a bond. It's strong after only a few days. But oh, is he stubborn! He would barely listen to any commands I gave him.

"Bulbasaur, do vine whip!"

It was like I was just saying, "stand there and blink!" And even though Dad has a young Nidoran, he (of course) has him trained for when to attack. And he was letting Bulbasaur attack first. So, we both just kind of stood there, waiting. Even though it was Dad, I was so embarrassed. How can I be good at this?

"You can't become a trainer in an afternoon, son."

Yeah, yeah, yeah. Of course, I can't. But I wish I could.

After about 10 minutes of the lamest stare-down ever, Dad put away Nidoran and we worked with Bulbasaur. Dad said I had to earn Bulbasaur's trust. He's got to believe in me.

How am I supposed to do that, though?!

Apparently, by bonding. So, Dad showed me some super secret tips on bonding with a pokemon. Which can be done by just spending time with them. Who would have thought? We walked around the house and played with some trees. I know it sounds crazy, but after an hour or so of doing that, I'd felt the bond between me and Bulbasaur grow a TON.

Dad interrupted around that time. "Let's give it another go. Then I bet your Mom will have dinner ready."

It's always about the food, right, Dad?

We stood in the makeshift battlefield Dad made a very long time ago. I felt... ready? Nidoran and Bulbasaur stood just yards from each other. "Bulbasaur, vine whip!" I yelled out. I was so nervous. It was the longest four seconds of my life... until Bulbasaur finally whipped those vines! Nidoran took a huge hit! We went back and forth for a while, until I could tell both Nidoran and Bulbasaur were very tired. I was opening my mouth to tell Bulbasaur to push out the finishing move when...

"Wait!" Dad yelled. "We're done here."

WHAT?! I was finally so close to winning my first battle! How could he tell me to stop?

"Why?!" I cried out.

"Because, we need to respect our pokemon. Look how tired they both are. This is not a battle for a gym badge. When we train as pokemon masters, our pokemon train, as well."

"We aren't here to fight them to complete exhaustion. It's time for a break."

I have to admit, I was so angry at first. I'd been so close to finally winning a battle! How dare he tell me that the fight was over? It's over when I say it's over.

After a few minutes, though, I calmed down. How could I be so mean? I love my Bulbasaur. I don't want him to be on the brink of death. I was being so selfish, and Dad was right.

We set up Bulbasaur and Nidoran with plenty of food and water to rest.

"I'm proud of you," Dad said. "You have made huge strides today. Now, I smell chicken from the kitchen. It's dinnertime!"

It is always about dinner, Dad....

THURSDAY

No training today. Dad says that if you constantly work on training, you'll become too obsessed, and your pokemon will suffer. He also says your social life will suffer, and since mine is already in shambles, I agreed to take a day off.

Surprisingly, I was able to avoid Scott all day. Hopefully, he wasn't training himself. I'm so paranoid that he's going to force a battle on me. I wouldn't be surprised. I think he only has a Pidgey, but if no one has seen him around town today... well, that has to mean he's up to something. I'm going to TRY to not worry about it.

And of course, how can I worry about Scott when I got to talk to Misty today? Oh, she's so pretty. I'm surprised I can even pay attention to our conversations. Sure, we were hanging out with other friends nearby... but I felt like she only had eyes for me. Or, am I being too hopeful?

"How's training with your dad going?" she asked.

We talked about training, and how I was so close to winning a battle, but that Dad stopped me.

"You know, I really think a lot of your dad," Misty said. "A lot of trainers get so wrapped up in winning, they don't think to actually care for and love their pokemon."

You know, I can see that. Even some of the most famous trainers don't seem to care for their pokemon. They just want to win big. How can anyone be that selfish? Pokemon are living creatures that we pledge to take care of. Not just so that we win the most badges.

I tell her this, and she gets this weird look on her face. Did her heart just flip-flop, too?

"I'm so glad you feel that way," she said. "I love my Squirtle like he's a part of the family. I couldn't bear to mistreat him."

She had a Squirtle?! I bet he'd be great friends with Bulbasaur.

We sat there and continued to talk for a little bit. She looked over my shoulder.

"There's a Pikachu walking by that tree..."

I whipped around. A PIKACHU?! It's rare to find one in our part of town.

He looked so playful. And I had pokeballs in my bag... but I didn't reach for one just yet. I remembered my training. I started to slowly get up, and quietly walked over to the Pikachu.

He noticed me... and he stopped. We looked at each other for a bit, and I felt a bond between us click. He was smiling.

I heard Misty from behind me. "Go for it!"

I reached for a pokeball... and the Pikachu stood still and smiled.

I tossed the ball... and I caught him. I caught a Pikachu!

"Oh, congrats!" yelled Misty. SHE HUGGED ME! Could this day get any better?

My pokedex continues get bigger; I've spent the whole day with Misty, AND I CAUGHT A PIKACHU.

I saw my group of friends walk over to where Misty and I were sitting. In a sea of congratulations, I only had eyes for Misty.

That gave me all the confidence I needed.

I'm going to bust my tail and train with Dad, and my first battle and win will be against Scott. But first... sleep.

FRIDAY NIGHT

24 hours later, and I am still shocked that I caught a PIKACHU. I came home, grinning from ear to ear, thrilled about my catch.

"You caught a WHAT?!" Dad replied when I told him. He was smiling just as hard as I was. "Using the training I taught you? Who would have thought, it's almost like I am a pokemon master or something."

Dad jokes. They're never funny. Even if your dad is a pokemon master.

Even Mom said she was proud of me. And she's never even caught a pokemon. She had a Vulpix as a kid, but only because it started following her. That Vulpix followed her home, and just stayed. She never wanted to battle – just loved her as a pet. Dad has always been the more fiery type. More competitive. But, he has never been that way with me. I've never seen anyone more patient than my dad.

I did it!

Mom's Vulpix

We had an awesome dinner, together as a family. I honestly cannot remember the last time we sat down and just laughed. No nagging, no rushing to appointments or work. If catching one pokemon made my family this happy, then I will work my hardest to be a pokemon master. Just like Dad. Maybe even better, but maybe I shouldn't push my luck, either. I usually can't walk down the street without getting a wet willy from Scott.

After dinner was cleared and the dishes were clean, Dad sat me down.

"I'm so, so proud of you," he said. "You have gotten such a strong start on this, you are going to be an amazing and strong pokemon master one day."

I wanted to cry, I was so happy.

"Now, go upstairs. We've got an early day tomorrow."

"WHAT?!" He's going to make me train on the weekends? I have to admit, though, his answer made me laugh.

"When I was your age, I was up on Saturday before the sun. I was determined to be the very best. And to catch the pokemon that roam at night. And usually, I was already out that late... spending time with your mom."

That's too much information, Dad.

But hey, it gives me an idea. Maybe if I can get enough courage to ask Misty out on a date (it has been crossing my mind lately...) we could go for a nighttime stroll and look for pokemon. She's already got five! She'd be totally prepared for a battle if a wild pokemon decided to fight back. Or, would I look like a pansy because I couldn't handle the situation myself? Maybe I'll hold off on the date idea...

I've never been big on girls... usually they're too prissy, with too much drama. But that changed when I met Misty last year. She's so strong and independent. She's like fire. And she says she likes water type pokemon, too. I refuse to believe she doesn't have a Charmander up her sleeve.

I'm writing this all before I go to bed. But, I'm so pumped. How am I going to sleep? All I can think about is training... and Misty.

But, I better try. I'd like to wake up before Dad uses his Squirtle to wake me up...

Saturday Night

I can't move.

I'm so TIRED. And I was right. Dad came in here with his Squirtle, who used his water jet to wake me up around 4:30 this morning. Still totally dark outside. I mean, I wasn't calling his bluff... but I thought he'd be a little bit nicer about waking me up.

After a quick breakfast, we were right at it. We battled with all of my pokemon, but not for a full battle. Only about ten minutes each. Then, we'd rest. He said this tactic allowed each pokemon to get used to their powers without them getting exhausted.

We took a break for a quick lunch, and then we were back at it. This time, Dad told me to pick one of my pokemon and prepare for a full battle. He wasn't going to tell me which pokemon he was going to pick, so I would have to use my wits if he picked a type that was stronger than my own.

It took me about five full minutes to decide. All of my pokemon had been working so hard this morning, and I wasn't exactly sure who to pick. Finally, I decided to go with Pikachu. He was looking the strongest, and even though my first battle was against my Dad... I didn't want to lose.

"Are you ready?"

I was so excited to hear those words.

"Pikachu... I choose you!"

I let him out onto the battlefield. I heard Dad from a few yards away... he went with Nidoran. "Pikachu... use thunderbolt!"

The battle started. Nidoran was strong, just as strong as Pikachu. It was an intense battle; we were constantly going back and forth. At first, I was worried Dad would go easy on me. But after awhile, I knew that he wasn't. Which I loved. I wanted a chance to prove myself.

Soon, it was clear the battle was almost over. The sun was setting... I hadn't realized how long we had been battling. I told Pikachu to give Nidoran a final shock with thunderbolt. He did... and Nidoran collapsed. I had won! I won my first battle.

Pikachu getting ready for thunderbolt

Against my legendary father.

He ran over to me and hugged me.

"I'm so, so proud of you! You did it!"

I'm positive that no matter how my pokemon training career goes, this will be one of my favorite moments.

"Now, I'm going to go take care of Nidoran. And you need to do the same with Pikachu. Even though he won, he's close to exhaustion. It's important to remember to take care of all of your pokemon after battles, even if they didn't fight," he said.

"Of course, Dad. I love Pikachu," I said.

He smiled. "Good. Clean up, and I bet your Mom has dinner ready."

Always about the food. Always.

Again, we had a great family dinner. I haven't seen Dad this happy in so long. Not saying that he wasn't a happy man before, but it's crazy to believe that I can make him this happy, just by going after my dreams.

It just so happens, we have the same dream. And now, we chase it together.

Dad says I'm ready for a battle OUTSIDE of the family. Maybe I do need to find Scott...

SUNDAY

Mom and Dad have always said that Sunday is the day of rest, so we didn't train today. Which is good, because I'm trying to plan a day this week when I can find Scott... and battle. Part of me is terrified. What if he beats all of my pokemon, then beats me up afterwards? What if Misty sees it? Is the social and physical rejection worth an attempt to put Scott in his place?

But, I've been working my tail off with Dad. And if one of the best pokemon masters in the world thinks I'm ready to battle a teenaged bully, then I have to believe in myself, too.

I met with some friends today, to catch up about training and what's been going on in their lives. Scott messes with all of them (though not as much as me), so they're pushing me to battle Scott.

"He needs to be put in his place!"

"You should just take one for the team. We all know you're the only one who's been training their pokemon."

Sure, we know that. But am I the one who should do it? Why am I suddenly the one who has to "take one for the team"?

Finally, I had to ask Dad about it. I really haven't told him about Scott, or even my feelings for Misty. I go to him for everything else, though, so why wouldn't I go to him about these problems?

"Whoa! That's a lot at once," he said when I told him about everything.

"First things first, let's deal with Scott," he said. "I could go to his parents and have them intervene. Which, I feel I might do anyways. I don't like bullies, I never have.... But, Son, you need to stand up for yourself. You are ready to battle him, I know you are. You're my kid! You are destined to become a champion," he said.

Well, I couldn't argue with that logic.

"I fully support you with this battle. You should find him this week, and challenge him," he said. "If he accepts, then show him who's boss. And, I know you will defeat him. If he doesn't battle you... then all of your friends will know that he's truly a coward."

Well, both options honestly sounded awesome.

"As for the girl..."

"Her name is Misty, Dad."

"Misty, yes... be honest with her. Tell her your feelings! She might surprise you. I had to take the horse by the reins with your mom. I was very open about my feelings for her from the get-go," he said.

"But what if she doesn't like me back?"

Dad hesitated. "Then, you know where you stand, and you can find someone else who wants to love the new pokemon champion."

He always has a way to put a smile on my face. And, he's right. I'd rather put my feelings up on the table and know, rather than be miserable and wonder. Feelings are messy and complicated. But Misty... she makes it all worthwhile.

Suddenly, I felt confident enough to battle Scott AND tell Misty how I feel. But not on the same day – I'm not Superman or anything. We'll solve one problem at a time.

First things first... tomorrow, I'm going to find Scott. And battle him. And kick his butt.

MONDAY NIGHT

Wow. Just wow.

I can't stop smiling. I just can't believe it. I had my first kiss today.

Yes, I said last night that I was going to find Scott and challenge him to a battle. But, I found Misty first. And she was crying. I rushed up to her and asked her what was wrong.

"Scott just bullied his way into a battle with me, and I thought I could take him," she said. "I only had my Starmie with me at the time. And he's evolved his Pidgey into a Pidgeotto. He's so strong!" she cried.

I felt two different emotions, very fast. First, I felt upset for Misty. Second, I felt angry. I don't think I've ever felt so angry in my life. How dare Scott bully someone into a battle, and then leave someone in tears? Plus, what kind of an idiot only has one pokemon and just trains it to evolve, rather than catching others?

I hugged her as she cried, and I told her I was so sorry. I asked what I could do, and she just looked at me. Without saying a word (and looking back, this could have ended badly), I just leaned in and kissed her. Just like in the movies. And she kissed me back!

"You like me, too!" she cried out. "I'm so happy! I didn't know how to tell you!"

At that point, I felt happier than when I beat Dad in my first pokemon battle. Misty likes *me* back!

"I was so scared to tell you," I told her. "But I'm so happy you feel the same way!"

"Well, now that we have figured that out, it's time to figure out a plan to put Scott in his place," said Misty. "He's got to go down, and while he's only got one pokemon, it's a strong one."

We sat for the longest time, coming up with different strategies for how to beat Scott. I shared what Dad had been teaching me, and Misty told me what her aunt has been teaching her on weekends. Misty's aunt is a gym leader in Celadon City.

Finally, the sun started to go down. We both needed to be at home.

"You can do it," she said. "I believe in you."

Those were all the words I needed to hear. We made plans to meet in the morning, and then look for Scott together. We kissed again, and then left. (Haha, I kissed a girl! Twice!)

I came home and immediately told Dad what happened this afternoon. He instantly got a smile on his face.

"Your first kiss! Now, when you beat Scott tomorrow, we'll really have a reason to celebrate!"

Always the over-achiever.

"Seriously, you have your strategies, you have your pokemon. We still have work to do, but you are more than capable of taking down this neighborhood bully with just one pokemon," Dad said.

"Now, let's get some of Mom's delicious food in you, and then it's off to bed. You've got a BIG day ahead of you, Son."

Well, you aren't wrong. You are never wrong, Dad. I'm ready for this day, though. Mostly to put Scott in his place and make him apologize to Misty... but also because I'm tired of the wet willies.

TUESDAY NIGHT

I only have two words for today.

Holy. Cow.

I did it. I won my first REAL pokemon battle. And it was against that jerk bully.

I woke up on my own this morning, no pokemon or Dad necessary. Mom made me a huge breakfast, but I didn't eat much. I was really nervous. Ready, but still nervous. I met with Misty (greeting her with a kiss, I have to add) and then we started to walk around. Scott usually hangs out on the north side of the field in town. And as usual, predictable Scott was exactly where we thought he'd be.

"What do you two losers want?" Scott asked as soon as we walked up.

As soon as he opened his big mouth, I started opening mine. "I'm tired of how you treat people," I said. "You need to apologize to Misty for how you treated her yesterday."

Scott looked shocked. I wasn't even standing up for myself, but I was standing up for Misty. "You are the biggest loser of them all," he said. "And you want me to apologize to your GIRLFRIEND? Get real."

That anger flashed back. "Then let's battle," I said.

To Scott, I guess I was full of surprises today. It looks as if my challenge threw him off guard. "Are you kidding me? I can beat all of your pokemon with my Pidgeotto. I don't care who your dad is," he said. "Let's do it, loser."

Scott pulled out his Pidgeotto. I was confident that Pikachu could take him down, without any help from Bulbasaur, Rattata, and Caterpie. But if needed, I could rely on them to take down this jerk of a bully, too.

"Pikachu, I choose you!"

Again, Scott looked shocked. I guess he hadn't heard about my newest addition.

"Pikachu, thunder shock!"

The battle began. I was really nervous the entire time, but with Misty behind me, I felt confident. And it felt like forever, but we finally came to the end of our battle. Scott looked tired, and honestly a little embarrassed. I looked at Pikachu, and he looked back at me. I could tell he was ready for more... and Pidgeotto was almost finished.

"Pikachu... give him one more shock of thunder!"

And in a flash of lightning... we were done. I had won.

I hugged Misty. She kissed me... in front of Scott! I looked out of the corner of my eye, and I saw Dad. He was smiling. He was watching me the whole time.

Scott looked at us. "Look, I'm sorry. I'm sorry for how I've been treating everyone. Misty, I'm sorry about yesterday and your Starmie. I didn't mean for it to go that far," he said. "No one likes a jerk. I'm really sorry."

Misty and I looked at each other, surprised. I hadn't even thought a battle would get Scott to apologize.

I looked back at him. "Do you think we could all be friends? It makes no sense to fight each other. We're all working towards becoming great pokemon masters. Why hate each other? We should be working together."

Again, Scott looked surprised. Then he smiled. "I'd like that," he said. "I'd like that a lot. Maybe your dad could share some tips?"

I smiled for a second, because I could hear Dad in my head. "I'm not teaching that punk a thing!"

But, I would change his mind. If I could have the ability to become friends with my own bully, I thought I could accomplish lots of things. Like becoming the best pokemon master in the world. It runs in the family.

To Be Continued...

Diary of a Pokemon Trainer 2 ➜ *http://amzn.to/2eOnUgp*

Diary of a Pokemon Trainer 3 ➜ *http://amzn.to/2fGk76e*

Thank you for reading *Diary Of A Pokemon Trainer 1*. I hope you enjoyed it! If you did…

1. Help other people find this by writing a review ➔
http://amzn.to/299oXBT

2. Sign up for my new releases e-mail, so you can find out about the next book as soon as it's available ➔
http://smarturl.it/PokemonGuide

3. Follow me at Amazon ➔
https://www.amazon.com/Red-Smith/e/B01LCO1O66

4. Which Pokémon do you want to meet? Comment in the review and I will get your favourite Pokémon's Diary out soon!

➔ *http://amzn.to/299oXBT*

Other Awesome Books by the Author

Gotta Grab'em All

Best-selling "Diary Of A Wimpy Pikachu" series

Diary of a Wimpy Pikachu 1 => http://amzn.to/2b0BfSC

Diary of a Wimpy Pikachu 2 => http://amzn.to/2bHJW52

Diary of a Wimpy Pikachu 3 => http://amzn.to/2bSqa6L

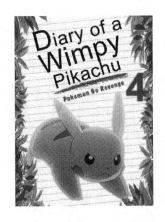

Diary of a Wimpy Pikachu 4 ➔ http://amzn.to/2cZgHb7

Diary of a Wimpy Pikachu 5 ➜ *http://amzn.to/2duuvNa*

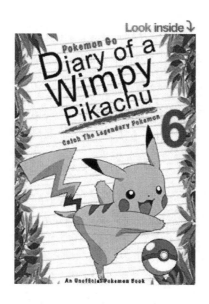

Diary of a Wimpy Pikachu 6 ➜ *http://amzn.to/2dbRkRX*

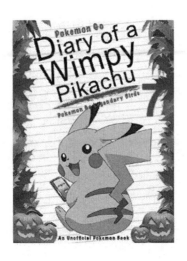

Diary of a Wimpy Pikachu 7 ➜ *http://amzn.to/2fpTUtV*

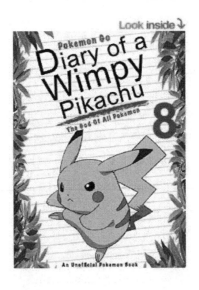

Diary of a Wimpy Pikachu 8 ➜ *http://amzn.to/2g0uzWW*

**SPECIAL EDITION➜ *Strange Origins of the Wimpy Pikachu*
1➜ *http://amzn.to/2c3ANCd*

***SPECIAL EDITION➜ *Strange Origins of the Wimpy Pikachu*
2➜ http://amzn.to/2djsEae

Diary of a Mythical Mew ➜ *http://amzn.to/2f623mU*

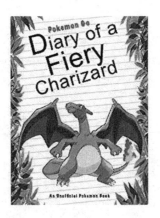

Diary of a Fiery Charizard ➜ *http://amzn.to/2e62lKa*

Diary of a Legendary Mewtwo ➔ *http://amzn.to/2dxdseJ*

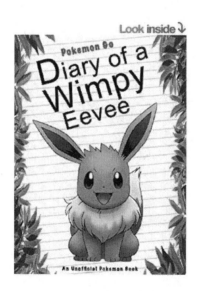

Diary of a Wimpy Eevee ➔ *http://amzn.to/2du9xQv*

Diary of a Farting Pikachu

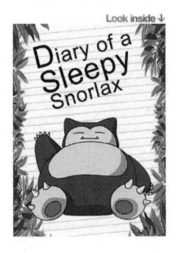

Diary of a Sleepy Snorlax

Diary of a Fiery Charmander

Download Here:

Diary of a Bulbasaur

Download Here:

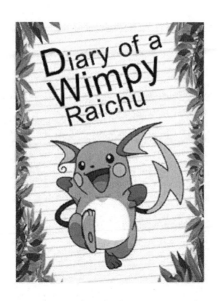

Diary of a Wimpy Raichu ➔ *http://amzn.to/2cZfOz2*

99 Amazing Facts that Will Blow Your Mind

Download Here: http://amzn.to/2bNeD4p

Want to learn the latest insider tips and secret guides on Pokemon Go?

I would highly recommend these books by author Adrian King

Pokemon Go: Art Of War ➔ http://amzn.to/2c40hAu

Pokemon Go: The Legendary Leveling Guide

Download Here: http://amzn.to/2brAxhm

If you like reading this, you might like this "Diary Of A Wimpy Super Mario" series too

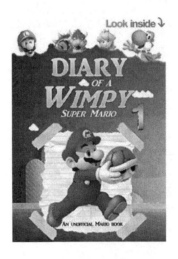

Get it here ➔ *http://amzn.to/2ejL6nT*

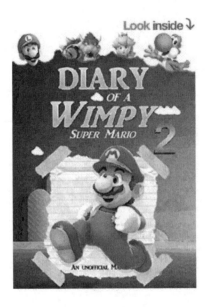

Get it here ➔ *http://amzn.to/2dFWls4*

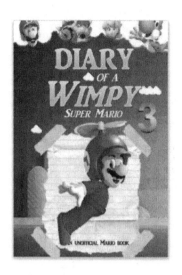

Get it here ➜ *http://amzn.to/2dqNNA5*

37899134R10037

Made in the USA
Middletown, DE
09 December 2016